This colourful book introduces young children to the idea of time in relation to things that they do, see and experience throughout a day.

For each hour, the pictures illustrate a variety of activities which could be taking place at that time. The text asks simple questions, designed to encourage discussion about the child's own experiences.

Available in Series 921

*† a for apple
*† let's count
* what is the time?
* shapes and colours

* *Also available in square format* Series S808 *and*
† *as* Ladybird Teaching Friezes

First edition

Published by Ladybird Books Ltd Loughborough Leicestershire UK
Ladybird Books Inc Auburn Maine 04210 USA

Printed in England (3)

what is
the time?

written by LYNNE BRADBURY
illustrated by LYNN N GRUNDY

Ladybird Books

What is the time?

It's 7 o'clock.

Time to wake up.
Wash your hands and face
and clean your teeth.

Can you get dressed by yourself?

What is the time?

It's 8 o'clock.

Time for breakfast.
You could have cereal or eggs
or toast or fruit?

What do you like to eat
for breakfast?

What is the time?

It's 9 o'clock.

Time to wash up.
Dry the spoons and cups.

How many plates?

Do you help to wash up
at home?

What is the time?

It's 10 o'clock.

Time to go out and play.
You could play with your toys,
or ride a bike, or play football?

What do you like to play?

What is the time?

It's 11 o'clock.

Time for a drink.
You could have milk or
orange juice?
Mum and Dad like coffee.

What do you like to drink?

What is the time?

It's 12 o'clock.

Time to help Mum and Dad.
Dad is working indoors.
Mum is cleaning the car.

Do you help at home?

What is the time?

It's 1 o'clock.

Time for dinner.
Everyone is hungry.
What is there to eat?

What is your favourite food?

What is the time?

It's 2 o'clock.

Time to go shopping.
We need to buy some food
and some new shoes.

Which shoes shall we buy?

Do you like going shopping?

What is the time?

It's 3 o'clock.

Time to go to the park.
You could play on the swings
or go down the slide?

What do you like to do in the park?

What is the time?

It's 4 o'clock.

Time to watch television
or look at a book.
Or you could draw a picture?

What is your favourite
programme on television?

What is the time?

It's 5 o'clock.

Today is special.
It's time for a party!
Lots of party food and games
to play with your friends.

Have you been to a party?

What is the time?

It's 6 o'clock.

Time to get ready for bed.
Get undressed and have a bath.
Then it's time for a story.

Do you have a favourite story?

What is the time?

It's 7 o'clock.